To
Maria Modugno

Copyright © 2018 by Holly Hobbie

All rights reserved. Published in the United States by Random House Children's Books,
a division of Penguin Random House LLC, New York.

Random House and the colophon are registered trademarks
of Penguin Random House LLC.

Visit us on the Web! randomhousekids.com

Educators and librarians, for a variety of teaching tools,
visit us at RHTeachersLibrarians.com

Library of Congress Cataloging-in-Publication Data is available upon request.
ISBN 978-1-5247-1863-3 (trade) — ISBN 978-1-5247-1864-0 (lib. bdg.) — ISBN 978-1-5247-1865-7 (ebook)

Book design by Martha Rago

MANUFACTURED IN CHINA
10 9 8 7 6 5 4 3 2 1
First Edition

Holly Hobbie

ELMORE

Random House  New York

Elmore lived by himself in an ancient maple tree. He loved it there.

Every few days he would climb down the huge
tree trunk as darkness fell to graze on his favorite
leaves and twigs. Then back he would go to his snug
hollow in the ancient tree.

Elmore was solitary—he lived alone—and
you would think he'd be used to that by now,
but here's the thing: he often felt lonely.
Solitude could be boring.

He'd always had trouble making friends. What was the problem? After all, the "L" in Elmore's name, his mother once explained, stood for "love."

He put up a sign:

He was discouraged by what he overheard:
"He's too prickly. It's hard to be around him."

Elmore shook his back, and his quills rattled.
It was true, if you got too close, you might get
needled, nettled, prickled. Elmore didn't mean
it. It just happened.

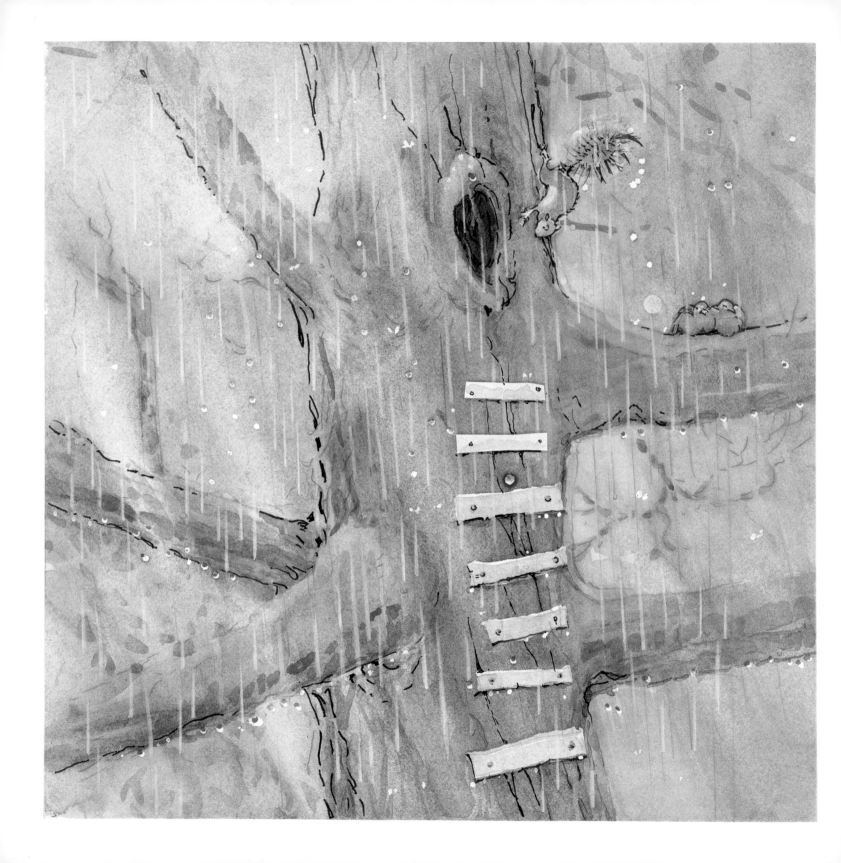

He spent a rainy day holed up in the
ancient tree, thinking about what to do.

What could be done about his trouble-
some quills? They were there to protect
him, like a coat of armor, but protect him
from what? Elmore's life was peaceful.
He was lucky.

The next day his old uncle happened to come shuffling along past Elmore's tree.

"Good morning, Elmore." A moment later he said, "You don't seem your usual cheerful self. Is something wrong?"

"I wish I didn't have all these quills," Elmore explained. "I'm too hard to be around. I have no friends."

"I'm your friend." His uncle smiled.

"That's different," Elmore replied.

"But you are a porcupine," his uncle stated emphatically. "You wouldn't be a porcupine without quills."

"I know," said Elmore. "I've got hundreds and thousands of them."

"You're a handsome porcupine," his uncle added. "Your quills are beautiful. You should treasure them."

His uncle's kind words made Elmore feel better.
Then, as he looked at the many quills scattered
about his cozy dwelling, he had an idea.

Elmore tied up each small cluster of
quills with a bit of string.

He posted another sign:

For two days they went like hotcakes.
Everyone could enjoy a quill pen, especially
if it was made from 100% real porcupine
quills—and free, too. They could make ink
from berries, Elmore suggested, which was
extra fun!

"Everyone loves getting a note from
a friend," he said as he handed out the
bundles.

By the time the last quill pens were
gone, Elmore was tuckered out, but most
of all he was happy.

In the days that followed, he received
all kinds of notes. It was exciting.

We Love our
QuiLL Pens.

THiS iS A picture
OF us.

Let's be Pen PaLs.

One bright morning after the quill event, there
was a big sign tacked to the trunk of Elmore's tree.